108

 P9-DID-851

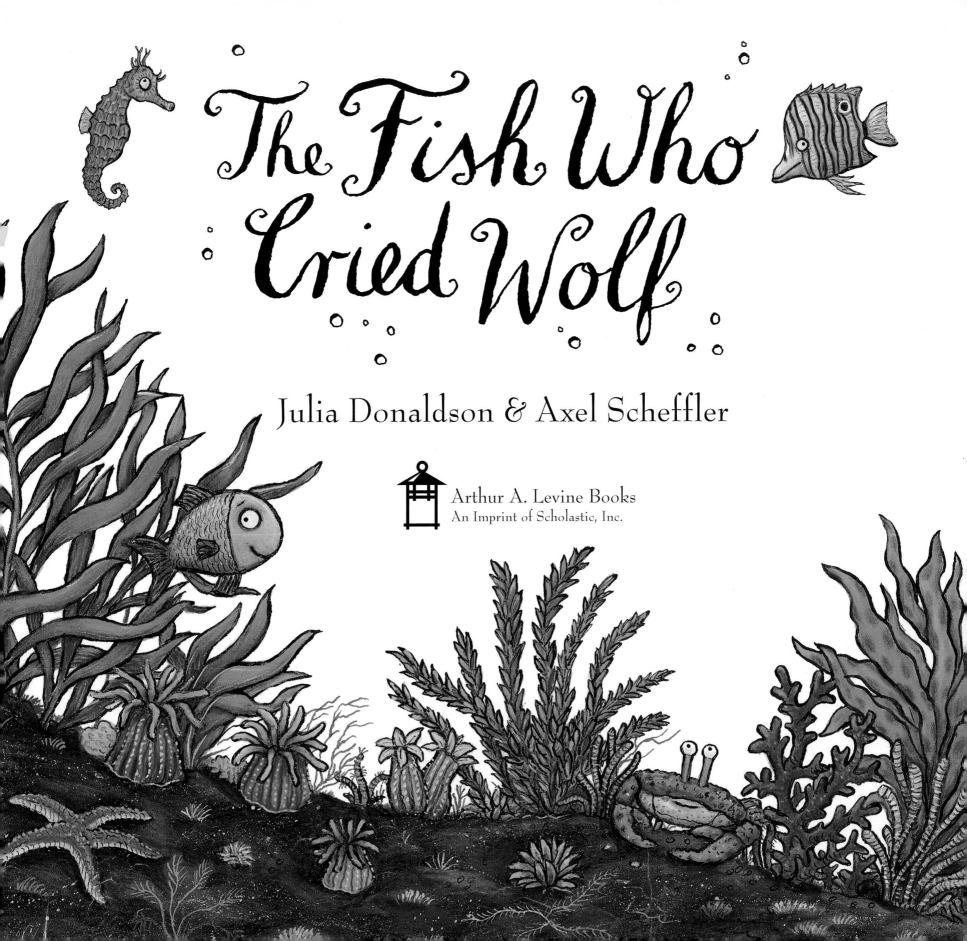

The Fish Who Cried Wolf

Julia Donaldson & Axel Scheffler

Arthur A. Levine Books
An Imprint of Scholastic, Inc.

Once there was a fish and his name was Tiddler.

He wasn't much to look at, with his plain gray scales.

But Tiddler was a fish with a big imagination.

He blew small bubbles but he told tall tales.

"Sorry I'm late. I was riding on a seahorse."

"Sorry I'm late. I was flying with a ray."

"Sorry I'm late. I was diving with a dolphin."

Tiddler told a different story every day.

At nine o'clock on Monday,

Miss Skate took attendance.

"Little Johnny Dory?"

"Yes, Miss Skate."

"Rabbitfish?" "Yes, Miss."

"Redfin?" "Yes, Miss."

"Tiddler? Tiddler?

TIDDLER'S LATE!"

"Sorry I'm late. I was swimming 'round a shipwreck.

I swam into a treasure chest, and someone closed the lid.

I bashed and I thrashed till a mermaid let me out again."

"Oh no she didn't." "OH YES SHE DID."

"It's only a story," said Rabbitfish and Redfin.

"Just a silly story," said Dragonfish and Dab.

"I *like* Tiddler's story,"
said Little Johnny Dory,

and he told it to his granny, who told it to a crab.

At nine o'clock on Tuesday, Miss Skate took attendance.

"Little Johnny Dory?" "Yes, Miss Skate."

"Spiderfish?" "Yes, Miss." "Sunfish?" "Yes, Miss."

"Tiddler? Tiddler?

TIDDLER'S LATE!"

"Sorry I'm late, Miss. I set off really early,
but on the way to school I was captured by a squid.
I wriggled and I struggled till a turtle came and rescued me."
"Oh no he didn't." "OH YES HE DID."

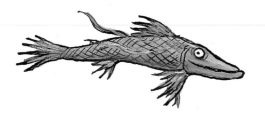   

"It's only a story," said Spiderfish and Sunfish.

"Just a silly story," said Devilfish and Dace.

"I *love* Tiddler's story,"
said Little Johnny Dory,

and he told it to his granny, who told it to a plaice . . .

. . . who told it to a starfish,

who told it to a seal,

who told it to a lobster,

who told it to an eel. . . .

At nine o'clock on Wednesday,
Tiddler was dawdling,
dreaming up a story,
his tallest story yet.

Lost inside his story,
he didn't see the fishing boat.

He didn't hear the fishermen.
He didn't spot . . .

... the
NET.

Meanwhile, in the schoolroom,
Miss Skate took attendance.
"Little Johnny Dory?"

"Yes, Miss Skate."

"Leopard Fish?" "Yes, Miss."

"Leaf Fish?" "Yes, Miss."

"Tiddler? Tiddler?

TIDDLER'S LATE!"

Ten o'clock . . .

. . . eleven o'clock. Still no Tiddler!

Twelve o'clock, lunchtime.
Where could he be?

Far away, the fishermen were
hauling in their fishing net. . . .

"This one's just a tiddler.
We'll throw it back to sea."

Tiddler was lost in the middle of the ocean
where strange lights glimmered . . .

. . . and strange fish flew.

He swam around in circles.

He shivered in the seaweed.
But then he heard a story,
a story that he knew. . . .

"Tiddler rode a seahorse.

Tiddler met a mermaid.

Tiddler met a turtle, who saved him from a squid."

Tiddler met a turtle, who saved him from a squid.

Tiddler found a shipwreck.

Tiddler found a treasure chest."

"Oh no he didn't."

"OH YES HE DID."

Tiddler peeped out and he saw a shoal of anchovies.

"Excuse me, can you tell me where you heard that tale?"

"We heard it from a shrimp,

but we don't know where *she* heard it."

And they took him to
the shrimp, who said,
"I heard it from a whale."

"I heard it from a herring."

"I heard it from an eel."

"I heard it from a lobster."

"I heard it from a seal."

"I heard it from a starfish."

"I heard it from a plaice."

The plaice said, "Just a minute, don't I recognize your face?"

"I'm Tiddler," said Tiddler.
"I'm tracking down my story."
The plaice replied, "I heard it from
my neighbor, Granny Dory."

One o'clock,

two o'clock . . . still no Tiddler.

Nearly hometime. Where could he be?

Just as the fishes were finishing their lessons . . .

IN SWAM TIDDLER
at half past three!

"Sorry I'm late but I swam into a fishing net.
I managed to escape, and I swam away and hid.
I was lost, I was scared, but
a STORY led me home again."
"Oh no it didn't." "OH YES IT DID."

 "It's just another story," said
Leopard Fish and Leaf Fish.

"Just a silly story," said
Butterfish and Blue.

 "It isn't just a story," said
Little Johnny Dory.

And he told it to a writer friend . . .
who wrote it down for YOU.

For Liam and his dad at the Bermuda Aquarium – J.D.

For Luca – A.S.

Text copyright © 2007 by Julia Donaldson • Illustrations copyright © 2007 by Axel Scheffler

All rights reserved. Published by Arthur A. Levine Books, an imprint of Scholastic Inc.,
Publishers since 1920, by arrangement with Scholastic Children's Books, London, England. SCHOLASTIC
and the LANTERN LOGO are trademarks and/or registered trademarks of Scholastic Inc.

No part of this publication may be reproduced, stored in a retrieval system, or transmitted in any
form or by any means, electronic, mechanical, photocopying, recording, or otherwise, without
written permission of the publisher. For information regarding permission, write to Scholastic Inc.,
Attention: Permissions Department, 557 Broadway, New York, NY 10012.

Library of Congress Cataloging-in-Publication Data

Donaldson, Julia.
The fish who cried wolf / by Julia Donaldson; illustrated by Axel Scheffler. — 1st ed.
p. cm.
Summary: Tiddler the fish is always telling tall tales about why he is late for school, but when he is
actually caught in a net and taken far from home, it is his stories that help him find his way back.
ISBN 0-439-92825-7 [1. Fishes—Fiction. 2. Storytelling—Fiction. 3. Stories in rhyme.] I. Scheffler, Axel, ill. II. Title.
PZ8.3.D7235Fi 2008   [E] — dc22   2007012308

ISBN-13: 978-0-439-92825-0 • ISBN-10: 0-439-92825-7

Book design by Leyah Jensen

10 9 8 7 6 5 4 3 2 1   08 09 10 11 12
Printed in Singapore • First edition, July 2008